Alex and the Drummer

A wonderfully typical experience with Autism!

WRITTEN BY

LAURA HALES

ILLUSTRATED BY

MYRAH SHARIFF

I've been playing my drum here for two years with no rest; rain or shine, snow or heat, I keep drumming. I stand outside a store that sells phones. I'm quite important, you know, but people tend to forget.

. . . I receive nothing.

No one sees me playing so strongly—keeping a steady rhythm through night and day.

4

Then, one winter day, a car slowly drives by. A boy with yellow hair and headphones over his ears eagerly looks and points my way.

"Momma! Look! Drummer!!"

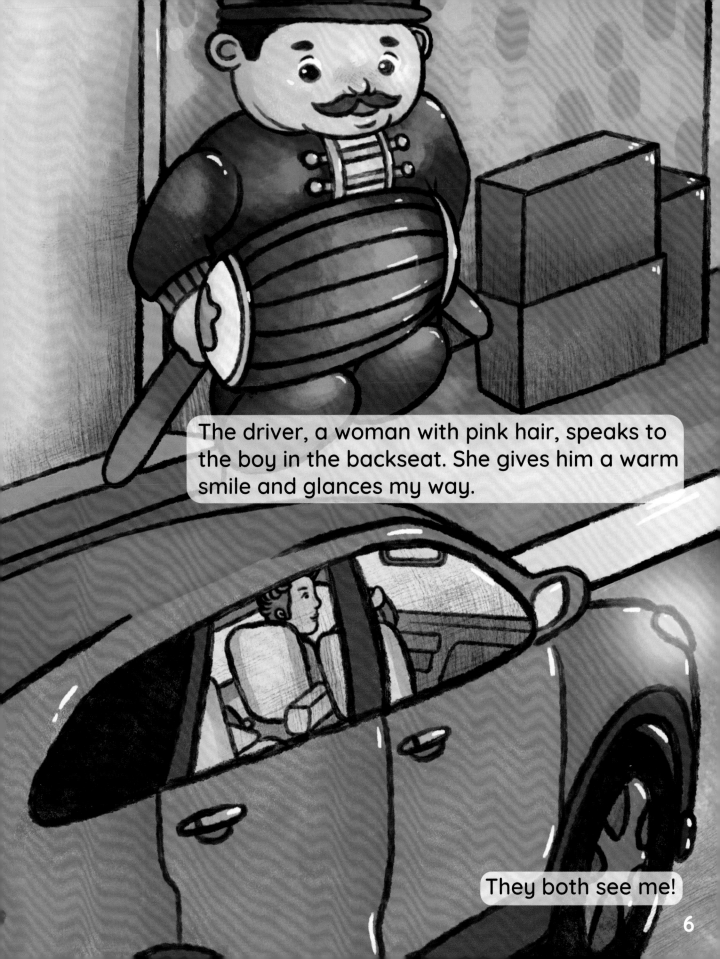

The driver, a woman with pink hair, speaks to the boy in the backseat. She gives him a warm smile and glances my way.

They both see me!

He claps . . .

. . . and shakes his hands with joy . . .

. . . as he waves goodbye.

The next day I see him again. And the day after. A big smile and wave through a lowered window.

Then,

without much thought on his part and too much thought on mine, he reaches out and pulls my plug from the wall.

Unplugged.

Unbearably slow, and all too quickly, I deflate to the cool February pavement—a melted snowman of fabric.

I watch as he uses my outlet to plug in a tool with a slithery black cord hanging from its end.

After two years of standing tall, striking my drum with almost no notice or appreciation,

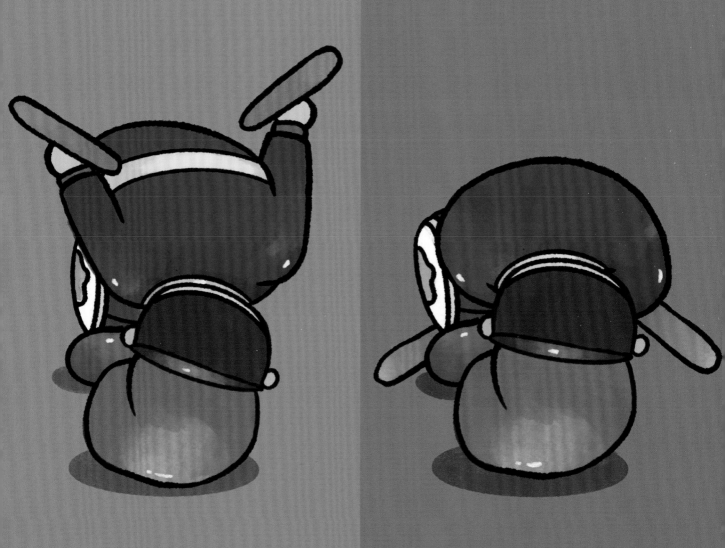

the show is over.

I lay in silent disappointment, my heart and my hopes as dashed as my drum.

Time passes, though how much I don't know. A few minutes? Hours? I'm unsure. Time loses meaning when you're so empty.

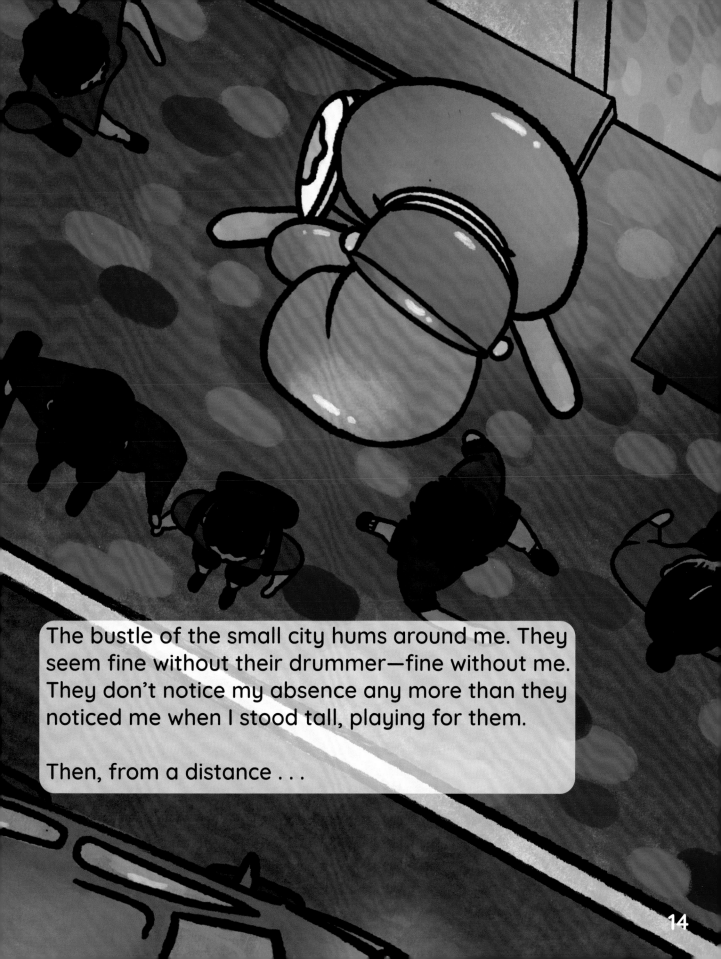

The bustle of the small city hums around me. They seem fine without their drummer—fine without me. They don't notice my absence any more than they noticed me when I stood tall, playing for them.

Then, from a distance . . .

"Oh, no Alex! The Drummer is sleeping today!"
The voice is anxious. Worried. I listen as she tries to
sound more cheerful.

"That's okay! I'm sure he'll wake up soon!"
She sounds brighter this time, but being an
expert on sound, I can still hear her panic.

Then another voice.
"Drummer fall down . . ."

I know this voice - the way he says his letter 'R.'
Could it be? My audience of one?

Oh my boy, I'm so sorry I've let you down. I try to lift my arms - to raise my sticks. I must play for him! But I can't do it.

What will he say?
My one fan . . . to see me like this. I'm so ashamed.
Please don't look, Alex. Not now.

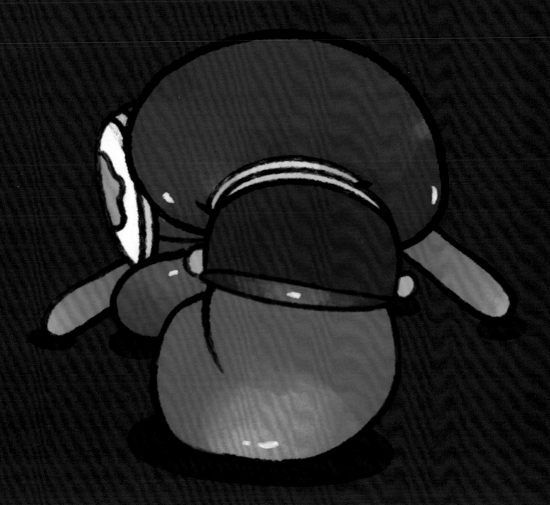

Without thought or care for chewed bubblegum or dog-stained cement, he lays down next to me. With me.

We stay for a moment—he and I—deflated. Lost from our routines on the unforgiving sidewalk, unsure how life could go on.

I'm aware of the driver's voice speaking to the working man. She seems to be explaining something and laughing nervously.

The pink-haired woman weeps as she takes photos of me with Alex.

21

Alex is so thrilled to finally meet his idol—and I'm always happy to take a photo with a fan.

Laura Hales
Author and Audiobook Performer

Laura is a mother of two on the Autism Spectrum. After living for 6 years in South Korea her family is recently returned to the United States. Laura's main goal in life is to bring self-acceptance and love to everyone she meets whether it's through her personal training or fitness classes, her free audiobooks she performs, her entertaining attitude or her publication of Alex and the Drummer.

Myrah Shariff
Illustrator and Designer

Ummairah (Myrah) Shariff is a self-taught illustrator who has been practicing art in its many forms since 2014. She mainly specializes in digitally creating children's book illustrations, but occasionally picks up the paintbrush too. Myrah's work is currently featured in non-profit organizations such as The Local Rebel and New Life Stories.